Jesus Said,

"Come, Follow Me"

Text © 2020 Cedar Fort, Inc.
Illustrations © 2020 Karina Matkevych
All rights reserved.

This is not an official publication of The Church of Jesus Christ of Latter-day Saints. The opinions and views expressed herein belong solely to the author and do not necessarily represent the opinions or views of Cedar Fort, Inc. Permission for the use of sources, graphics, and photos is also solely the responsibility of the author.

ISBN 13: 978-1-4621-3783-1

Published by CFI, an imprint of Cedar Fort, Inc.
2373 W. 700 S., Springville, UT 84663
Distributed by Cedar Fort, Inc., www.cedarfort.com

Library of Congress Control Number: 2020933650

Cover design and typesetting by Shawnda T. Craig
Cover design © 2020 Cedar Fort, Inc.

Printed in the United States of America

10 9 8 7 6 5 4 3 2 1

Printed on acid-free paper

Jesus Said, "Come, Follow Me"

illustrated by Karina Matkevych

written by Molly McNamara Carter

CFI • An imprint of Cedar Fort, Inc. • Springville, Utah

When Jesus was on the earth,
He showed the way to be.
He followed God's commandments
and said, "Come, follow me."

On a stormy day,
Jesus calmed the sea,
then turned to His disciples
and said, "Come, follow me."

Jesus taught by His example.
He loved the sick and suffering.
He blessed them to be well
and said, "Come, follow me."

Jesus forgave everyone,
no matter what their sin may be.
He taught forgiveness is for all
and said, "Come, follow me."

The people followed Jesus.
He fed all that were hungry,
with two fish and five loaves,
and said, "Come, follow me."

Jesus's disciples saw Him
walking on the sea.
He told them not to be afraid
and said, "Come, follow me."

Jesus healed the people
in a place called Galilee.
He raised a girl from the dead
and said, "Come, follow me."

Jesus healed the lepers.
From disease they'd now be free.

He told them to tell others
and said, "Come, follow me."

Jesus healed the blind man.
He blessed him so he could see.

He told him to have faith
and said, "Come, follow me."

Jesus gathered the children
and took them on His knee.
He cared for them and loved them
and said, "Come, follow me."

Because He loved all people,
He suffered in Gethsemane.
He paid for everyone's mistakes
and said, "Come, follow me."

When Jesus was resurrected,
He returned to Galilee.
He showed them scars on His hands and feet
and said, "Come, follow me."

Jesus loved the people,
just like you and me.

Jesus cares for all of us
and says, "Come, follow me."